Imagine a very dangerous dragon.

Sort of like this.

For Nikolai and Bruno

Ute Krause

Oscar
and the
Very Hungry
Dragon

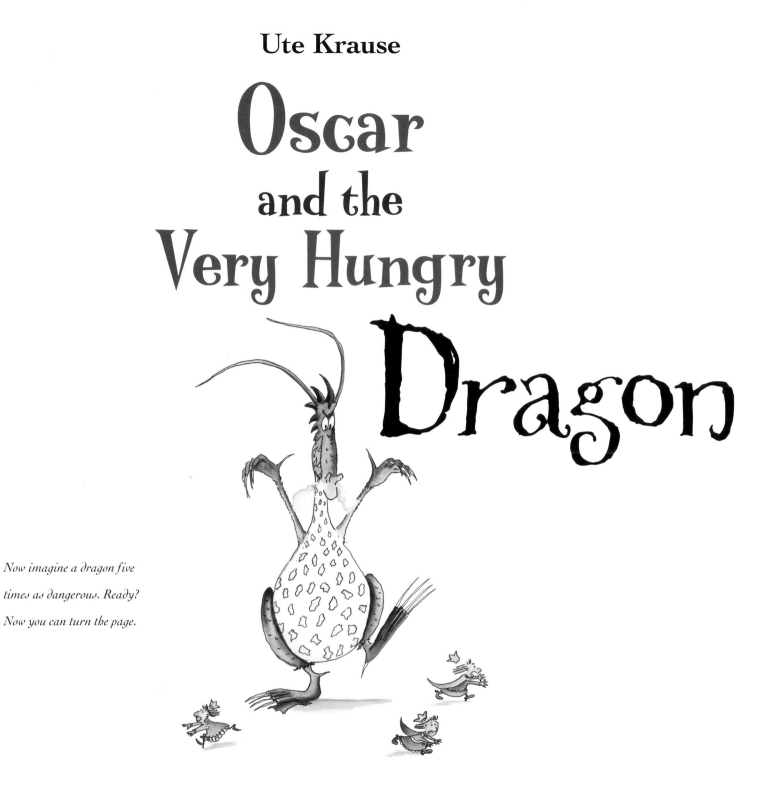

Now imagine a dragon five

times as dangerous. Ready?

Now you can turn the page.

NorthSouth
New York / London

The earth shook and trembled. The great dragon was awake and very hungry. It was time to feed him a princess. But no princess was available.

So the next best thing was to give him a child.

Mr. Ballymore, the village elder, had all the children write their names on pieces of paper and put them in a hat. He shook the hat, then picked a name. Oscar!

Oscar had to go and meet the dragon. His mom wept bitterly.

It took Oscar hardly any time to find the dragon, who was eagerly awaiting him and very, very hungry. He hadn't eaten for 344 days. But when he saw Oscar, he was disappointed. He had hoped for a fat, juicy princess.

"Why, you're not even a teeny-weeny snack!" he roared.

Oscar held his nose. The dragon had really bad breath after his long fast.

Oscar knew he couldn't run away, so he had to think of a clever answer really fast.

"If I were you," he said, "I'd fatten me up and turn me into a main course."

The dragon considered Oscar's suggestion. "Not a half bad idea," he growled. He swept Oscar up and carried him off to his lair.

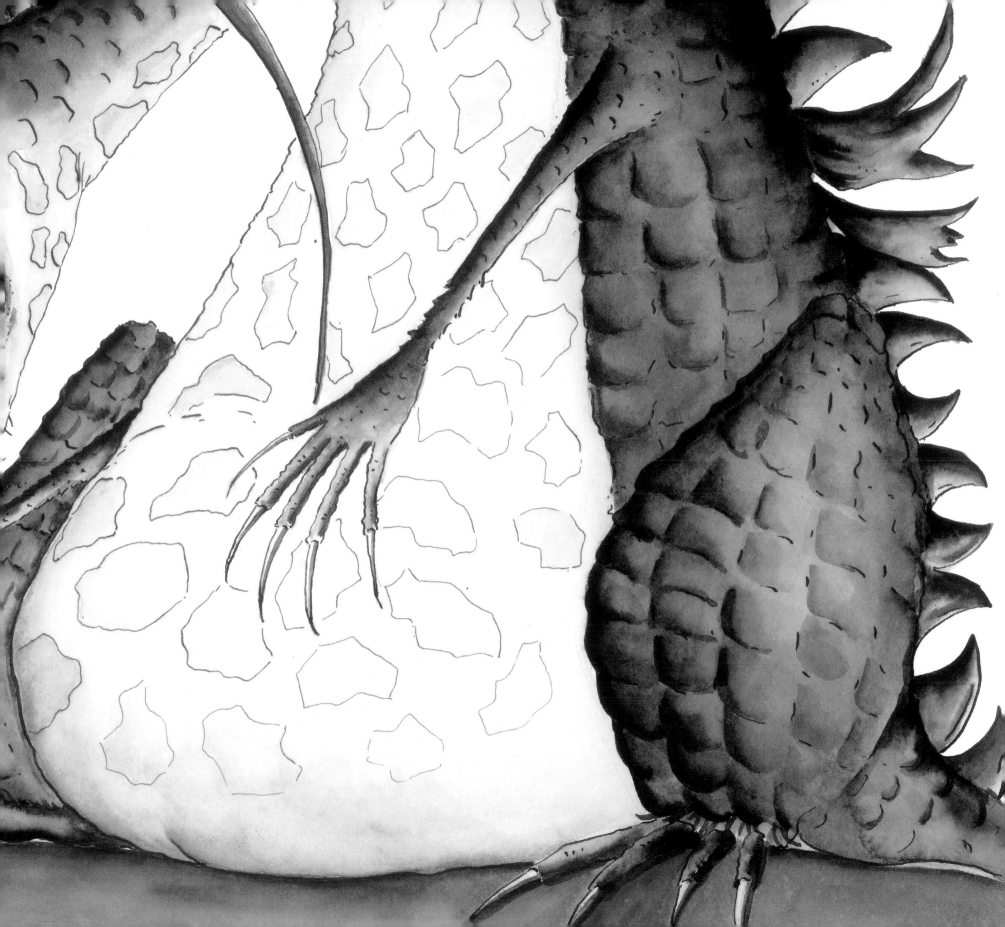

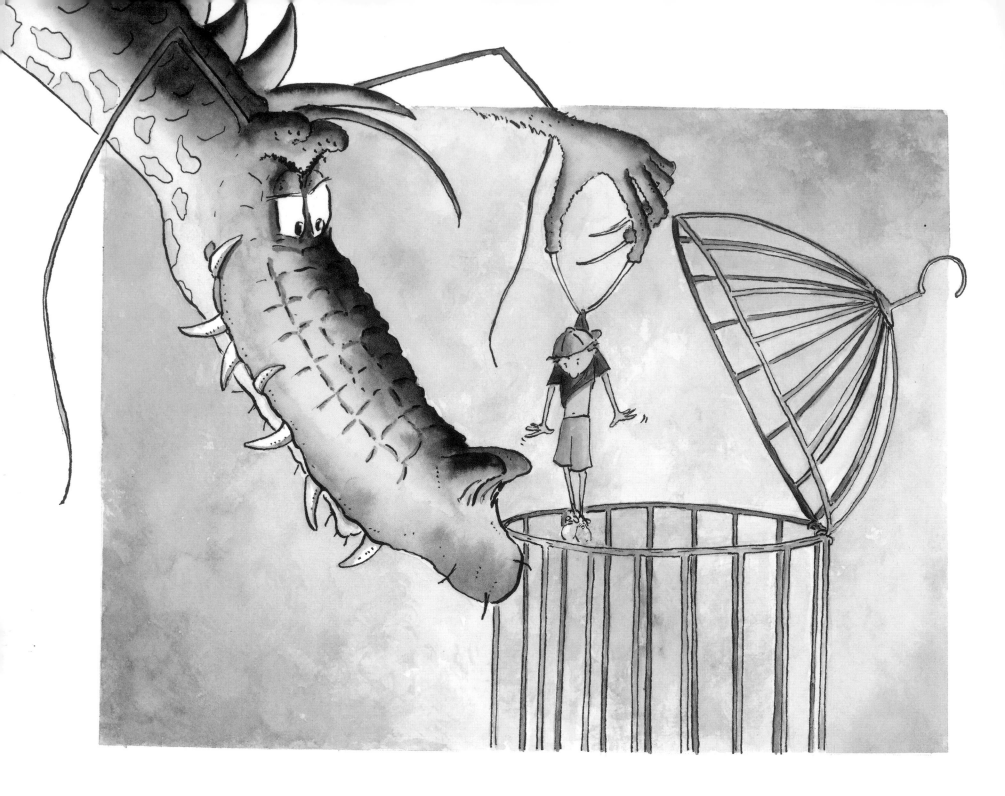

The dragon plunked Oscar in a cage. "What do you need to fatten up?" he asked.

Oscar wrote out a long shopping list and ordered a professional cooking stove.
When the dragon returned with all the goodies, Oscar immediately set to work on
a wonderful meal.

Very soon the most delicious smells came wafting through the cave. Oscar's mom had taught him a thing or two.

"Dinner's ready," he called. "Grilled eggplant for starters, then pasta and homemade ice cream."

"SHUT UP!" roared the dragon. "Dragons don't eat stupid human food." He hunched over his growling belly and tried his best to ignore Oscar, who was enjoying his lovely meal.

The next morning Oscar handed the dragon a new shopping list. It was three times as long as the list from the day before.

The dragon returned with all the groceries. Soon the smells that filled the cave made his mouth water. He could feel his empty belly rumbling like a steam engine.

"NOOO!" he yelled when Oscar offered to share his meal.

Every day the shopping list grew longer and longer and Oscar's cooking grew better and better. He made the most amazing dishes. The poor dragon grew dizzy with hunger, but he continued to refuse Oscar's offer.

"NOOO AND NOOO AGAIN!" he roared.

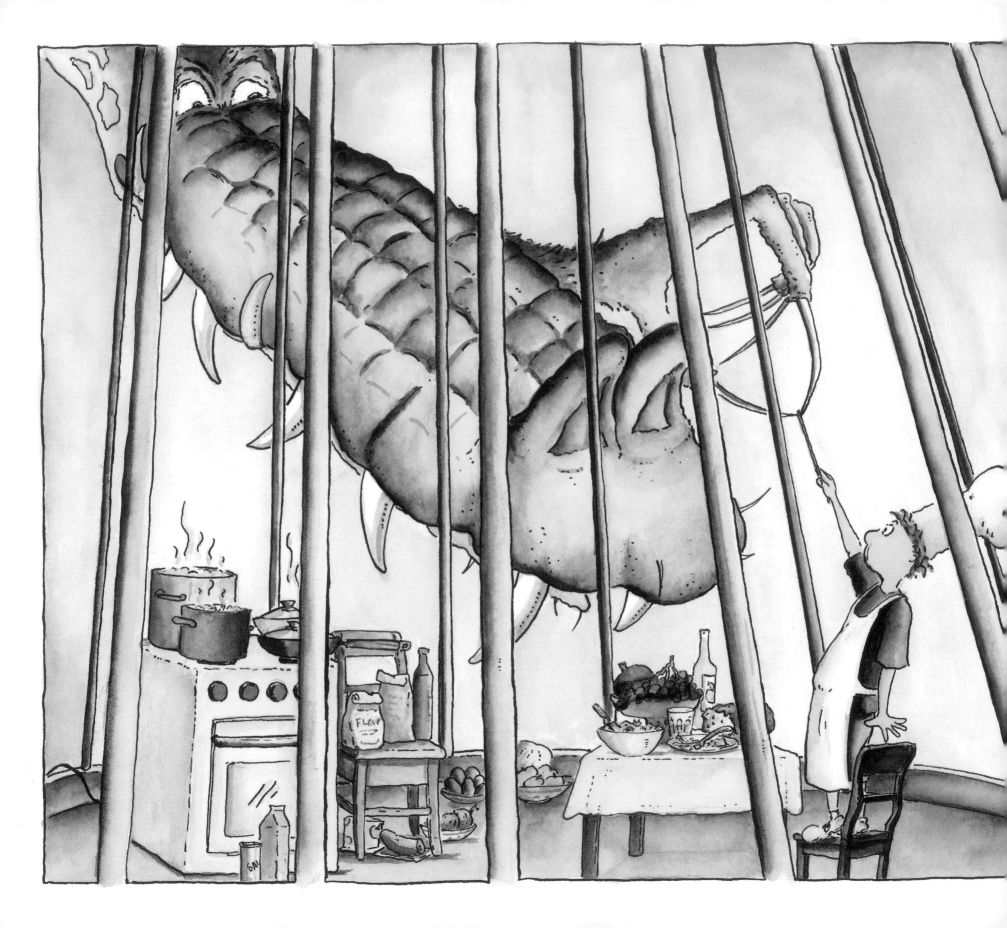

He roared so loudly that the villagers heard him. "Oscar's done for," they cried, wiping their eyes sadly. "He was such a nice boy."

Oscar's belly was getting nice and round with so much food.

"Show me your finger," said the dragon one day. "I want to check if you've gained weight."

Oscar, who had learned a thing or two from listening to fairy tales, quickly held out the cooking spoon to the nearsighted dragon. The dragon felt it and shook his head in disappointment.

"This is too skinny to fill even the belly of an ant," he said.

"Well, I have some leftovers," said Oscar to comfort the poor dragon.

"NOOO—" The dragon began to roar, but then his voice cracked and he had to lean against the wall. He had grown so weak with hunger. "Well," he added in a small voice, "on the other hand, it would be a waste of food *not* to eat them, wouldn't it."

"Yes, it would," said Oscar, and he began to dish up the leftovers. The dragon, who had only eaten princesses so far, was amazed when he tasted Oscar's cooking. In fact, he liked it so much, he wanted more and more. And when the last plate was licked clean, he fell into a deep, happy sleep. (He snored so loudly, Oscar didn't sleep a wink.)

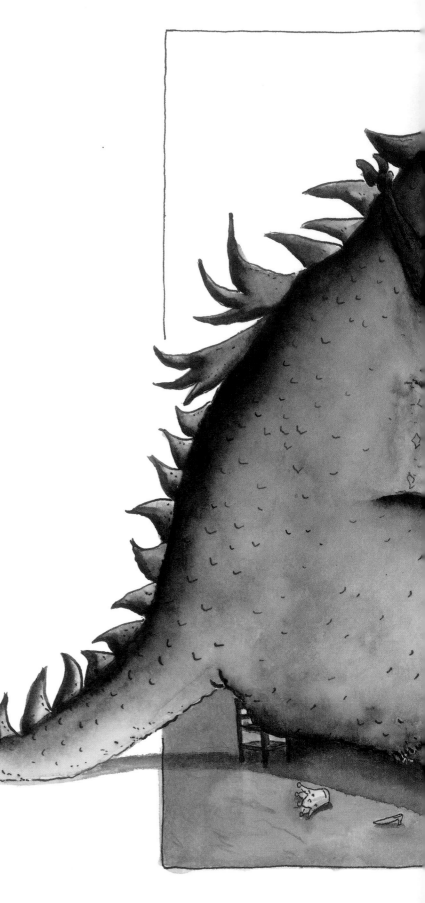

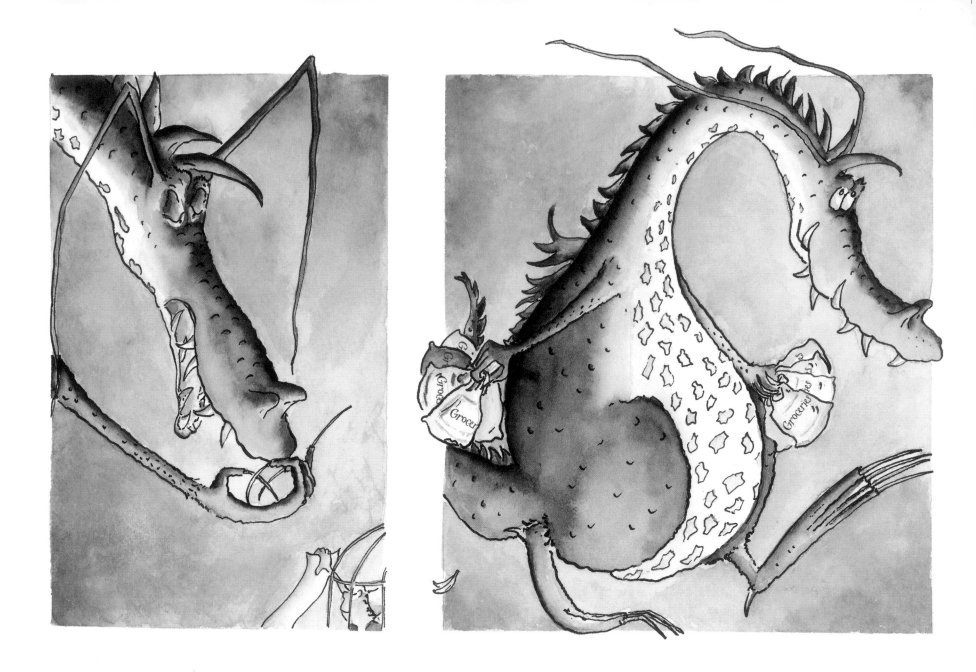

"You may as well cook for me too," said the dragon the next morning when Oscar handed him the shopping list.

Oscar outdid himself that day: asparagus soup, followed by filet mignon on a bed of young beans, with a crêpe suzette to top it off. The dragon was amazed, though of course he didn't show it, and from that day on Oscar cooked for both of them.

As the smells came wafting down into the village, Oscar's mother cried, "He's alive! Oscar's alive! I recognize those smells! I taught him how to cook that dish!"

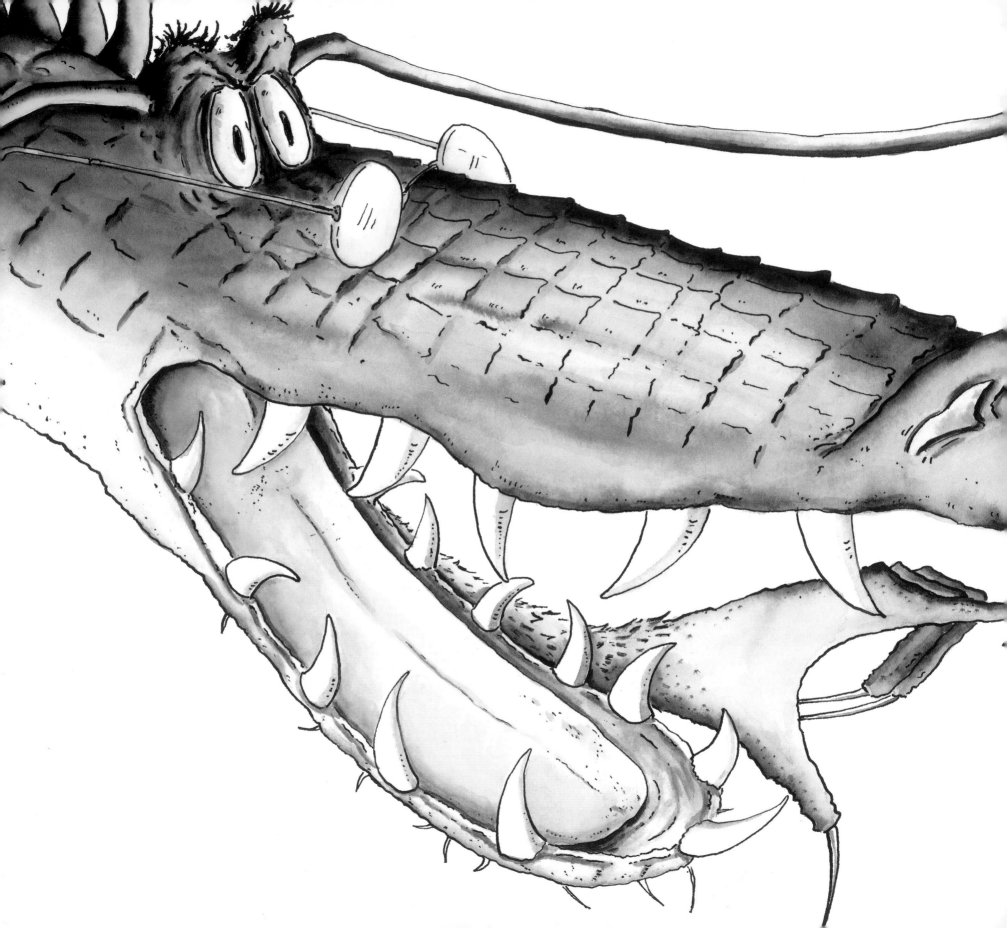

So time passed, until it occurred to the dragon that he hadn't checked Oscar's weight for a long time.

"Show me your finger," he said. Oscar, who was busy cooking, held up a stick. He didn't bother to look at the dragon until it was too late!

The dragon had been to the optician and gotten himself a brand-new pair of glasses. Angrily, he stared at the stick and at Oscar, who had gotten very chubby.

"YOU TRICKED ME!" he roared. "You'll pay for that. You are going to be my next main course."

He made a grab for Oscar. Oscar jumped aside, but . . .

. . . he wasn't quick enough. The dragon held him tight between his claws, ready to swallow him whole.

"Wait!" cried Oscar. "Think before you act! If you eat me now—fine. You'll have one good meal. But never again will you have double-layered chocolate cakes, fudge sundaes, coconut creams, or meringues. Not to mention chocolate chip cookies, banana splits, blueberry pies . . ."

The dragon's mouth watered. "Well, that's a thought," he said grumpily. "Still, you tricked me and—"

"Look," Oscar interrupted. "I promise I'll stay and cook for you if you promise not to eat me."

"I'll have to think about that," muttered the dragon, but actually he already knew that eating Oscar would be a real waste. "All right," he said, pouting a little.

"One more thing," Oscar added. "My birthday's coming up, and I want to invite my family and all my friends."

"All right," said the dragon. "Let's go."

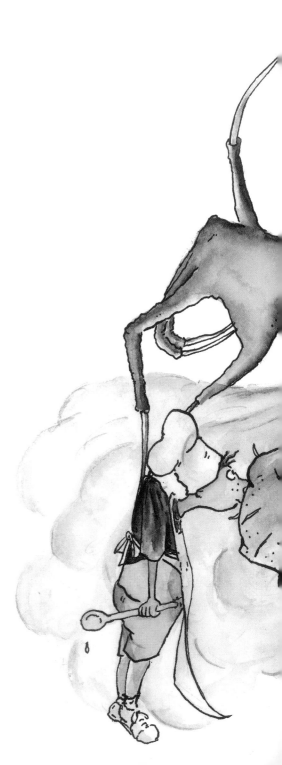

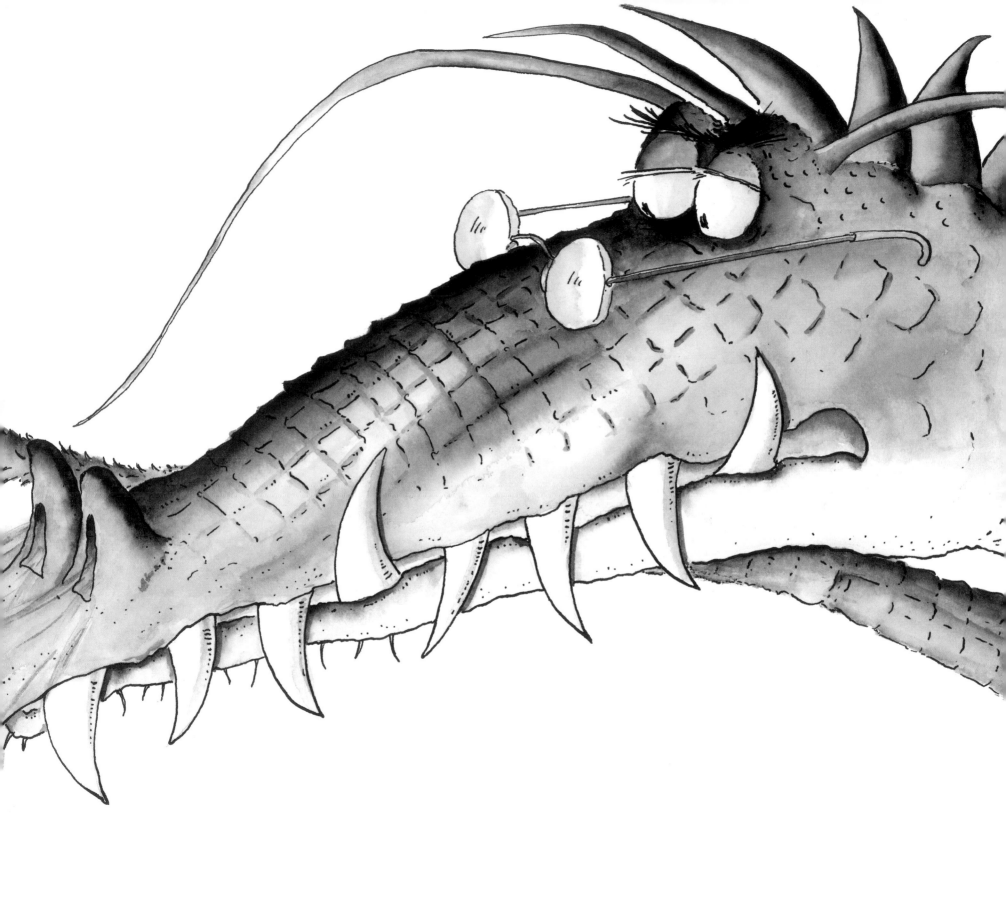

When they reached the village, nobody was there. Everyone was hiding from the dragon— everyone except Oscar's mother. She was very happy to see her son.

When the other villagers saw that the dragon was just chatting and being social, they came out of their hiding places and joined in.

Everyone came to the party at the dragon's den.
They all brought something to eat. It was the best
birthday party Oscar had ever had. The dragon ate
his way through all the dishes, took the kids for rides
on his back, and when it grew dark, made the most
fantastic fireworks anyone had ever seen.

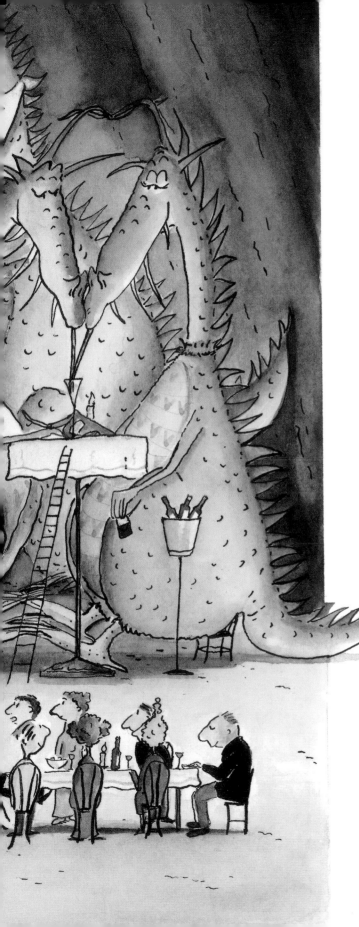

Oscar kept his promise and stayed with his new friend. Together they opened a five-star restaurant. And together they invented the most amazing dishes anyone had ever tasted.

First published in the United States, Great Britain, Canada, Australia, and New Zealand in 2010
by North-South Books Inc., an imprint of NordSüd Verlag AG, CH-8005 Zürich, Switzerland.
Distributed in the United States by North-South Books Inc., New York 10001.

Library of Congress Cataloging-in-Publication Data is available.
ISBN: 978-0-7358-2306-8 (trade edition)
Printed in China by Leo Paper Products Ltd., Heshan, Guangdong, March 2010.
1 3 5 7 9 ◉ 10 8 6 4 2

www.northsouth.com